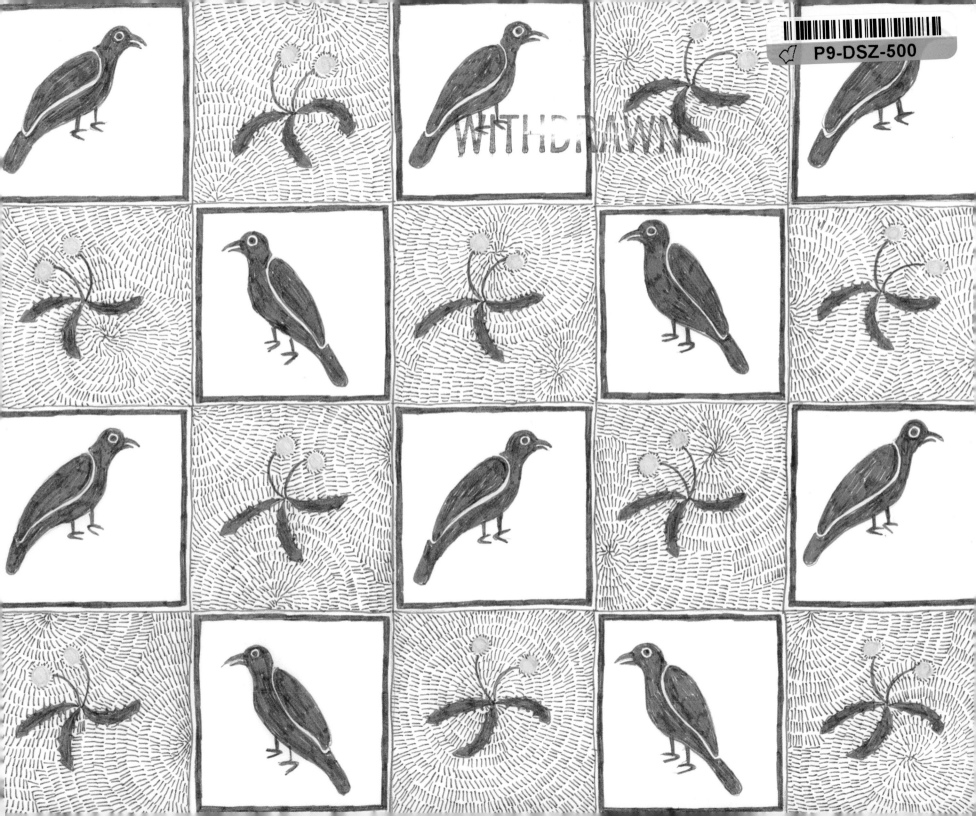

For Uta, Kiki, and Zadie

Ninja Boy's Secret

by Tina Schneider

TUTTLE Publishing

Tokyo | Rutland, Vermont | Singapore

About Tuttle "Books to Span the East and West"

Our core mission at Tuttle Publishing is to create books which bring people together one page at a time. Tuttle was founded in 1832 in the small New England town of Rutland, Vermont (USA). Our fundamental values remain as strong today as they were then—to publish best-in-class books informing the English-speaking world about the countries and peoples of Asia. The world has become a smaller place today and Asia's economic, cultural and political influence has expanded, yet the need for meaningful dialogue and information about this diverse region has never been greater. Since 1948, Tuttle has been a leader in publishing books on the cultures, arts, cuisines, languages and literatures of Asia. Our authors and photographers have won numerous awards and Tuttle has published thousands of books on subjects ranging from martial arts to paper crafts. We welcome you to explore the wealth of information available on Asia at **tuttlepublishing.com**.

Published by Tuttle Publishing, an imprint of Periplus Editions (HK) Ltd

www.tuttlepublishing.com

ISBN 978-4-8053-1526-2

Distributed by

North America, Latin America & Europe
Tuttle Publishing
364 Innovation Drive,North Clarendon, VT 05759-9436 U.S.A.
Tel: 1 (802) 773-8930; Fax: 1 (802) 773-6993
info@tuttlepublishing.com; www.tuttlepublishing.com

Japan
Tuttle Publishing
Yaekari Building 3rd Floor, 5-4-12 Osaki, Shinagawa-ku, Tokyo 141-0032
Tel: (81) 3 5437-0171; Fax: (81) 3 5437-0755
sales@tuttle.co.jp; www.tuttle.co.jp

Asia Pacific
Berkeley Books Pte. Ltd.
3 Kallang Sector, #04-01, Singapore 349278
Tel: (65) 67412178; Fax: (65) 67412179
inquiries@periplus.com.sg; www.tuttlepublishing.com

21 20 19   10 9 8 7 6 5 4 3 2 1

Printed in China   1905RR

Ninja Boy did not want to be a ninja. He did not want to be as still as a stone.

He wanted to play sonatas to inspire tulips to sing, and the wind to dance through open windows like green grass happiness.

...to learn stealthy skills

like SHAPE shifting and the art of being invisible.

Ninja Boy's Dad was a ninja. He did not play the violin.
He spent his days meditating. His mind was so
still that he could see the movement of molecules
that danced inside everything solid and motionless.

His Dad was quiet, like a mountain waiting in winter. His gaze was fixed upon his son. His eyes were harder than glass.

For a long time Ninja Boy was frozen under his father's stare.

His mind was as blank as white paper.

BOW

END SCREW — BOW GRIP — STICK — FROG — EYELET — HAIR — TIP

But suddenly he knew exactly what to do.
He took out his violin and rested it on his shoulder.
He perched his bow gently on the strings.

VIOLIN

SCROLL — TUNING PEG — NECK — FINGER-BOARD — STRINGS — BELLY — THE BRIDGE — F HOLE — CHIN REST — END BUTTON

He closed his eyes, took a deep breath...

...and then Ninja Boy

l e a p t

from his Dad's

S I L E N C E

into

MUSIC

HE PLAYED
QUIETLY
AT FIRST
LIKE A WHISPER.

The trees leaned into support him.
The grasses sang out with encouragement.
And as he played Ninja Boy's confidence grew.

He played the only song he could.
He played the song in his heart.

His fingers knew the way.
His breath kept the tempo.

Soon his song filled every corner of the house with joy.

Swooping and gliding on the air.

When his song ended Ninja Boy slowly opened his eyes. He could hardly recognize his Dad. The little lines around his Dad's eyes crinkled with delight. The corners of his lips curled with approval.

The End

Arpeggio:
(ar-<u>pe</u>-ji-o)
a chord in which the notes are played one after the other instead of at the same time.

Concerto:
(kən-<u>cheIr</u>-to)
a musical piece for solo instruments and an orchestra, usually with three or more contrasting movements.

Harmonize:
(<u>har</u>-mə-naIz)
to play or sing different musical notes at the same time that sound nice together.

Meditate:
(<u>me</u>-di-teIt)
to clear the mind for a period of time as a way to find peace.